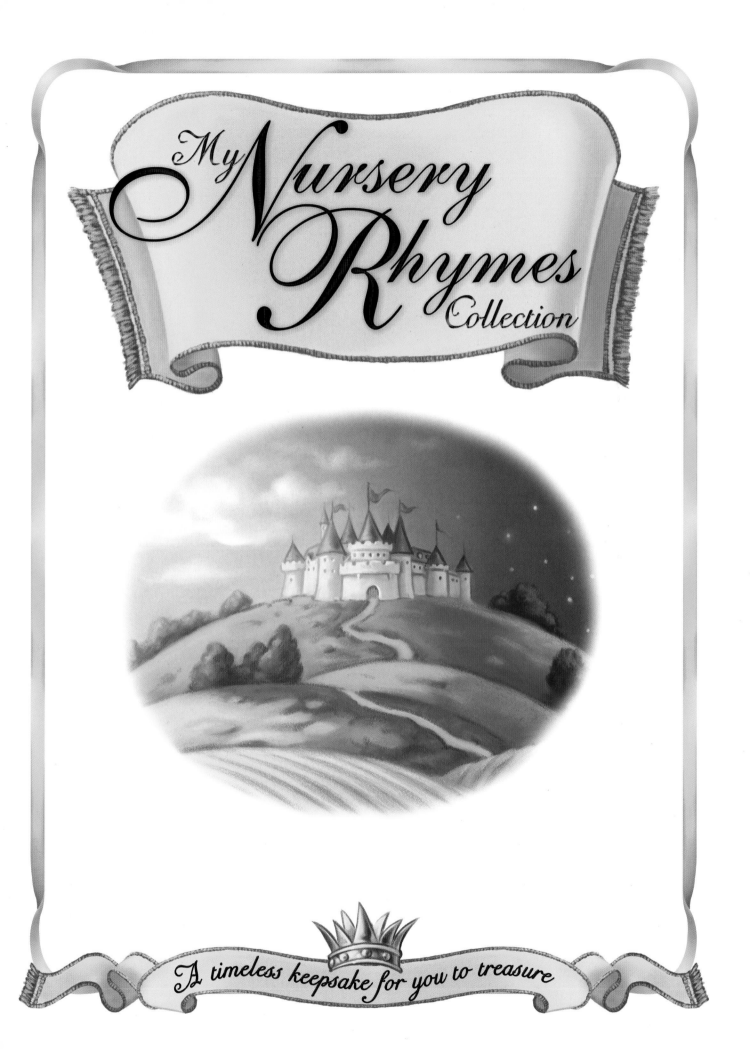

My Nursery Rhymes Collection

A timeless keepsake for you to treasure

My Nursery Rhymes Collection
Published in 2008 by Hinkler Books Pty Ltd
45–55 Fairchild Street
Heatherton Victoria 3202 Australia
www.hinklerbooks.com

© Hinkler Books Pty Ltd 2006

Editor: Karen Comer
Project Manager & Designer: Sonia Dixon
Cover Illustrator: Anton Petrov
Illustrators: Andrew Hopgood, Melissa Webb, Gerad Taylor,
Geoff Cook, Bill Wood, Anton Petrov and Marten Coombe
Art Director: Silvana Paolini

Prepress: Splitting Image

3 5 7 9 10 8 6 4 2
10 12 13 11 09

ISBN: 978 1 7418 2936 5

Printed and bound in China

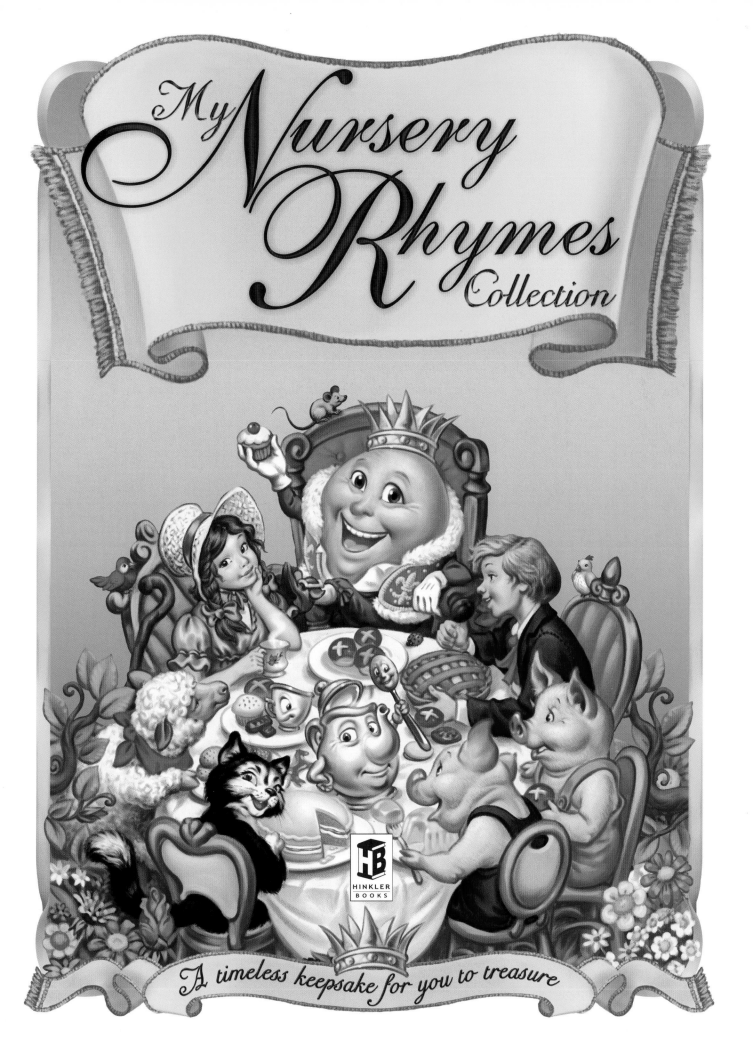

My Nursery Rhymes Collection

A timeless keepsake for you to treasure

HB
HINKLER
BOOKS

Reading opens up doors to different worlds. Reading provides children with a firm grasp of language so they can express their needs, stories and dreams. Reading encourages children, and the adults they will become, to communicate passionately and compassionately, succinctly and appropriately. Ultimately language is the key to communication, and communication is the key to relationships — both personal and professional.

A common language of nursery rhymes creates a shared vocabulary between parents and children. It is great fun to make all the animal noises for 'Old McDonald had a farm' and easy to identify with hungry Jack Horner. It's comforting to be tucked into bed with the words from 'I see the moon' and amusing to laugh at Humpty Dumpty falling down. Nursery rhymes are the beginning of language — they will help to foster a love of rhyme and nonsense. Children can experience the flow of language and sounds, as well as gain an understanding of different situations and emotions.

Nursery rhymes are meant to be read aloud — loudly and enthusiastically. They also inspire action. Children love actions — using their fingers for 'Twinkle, twinkle little star', and using their whole body for 'I'm a little teapot' helps them to link the words to the actions, coordinating body, mind and spirit.

Different rhymes suit various purposes at each stage of a child's life. 'Moses supposes' has relevance for a baby just discovering its toes; the lullabies, of course, are appropriate for bedtime; and many of the rhymes about food can be remembered when preparing meals or encouraging a child to eat. Substitute your child's name in a rhyme, for example, 'Pat-a-cake' — 'Put it in the oven for (Thomas) and me'. Rhymes are short enough to lend themselves to first dramatic performances — a simple rendition of 'Baa, baa black sheep' can be performed by a group of three year olds. The classic rhymes, the ones you can remember easily, are perfect for entertaining children during car trips.

The time taken to sit with a child on your knee and read a handful of nursery rhymes is invaluable. The cuddles, looking at pictures and repeating words, sharing a giggle and a new discovery, creates bonds that will last, even when discussing chores over the kitchen table!

Happy reading,

Karen Comer
Editor

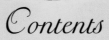

Contents

Contents

Contents

Wriggle Your Hips

The Dog Made A Bow

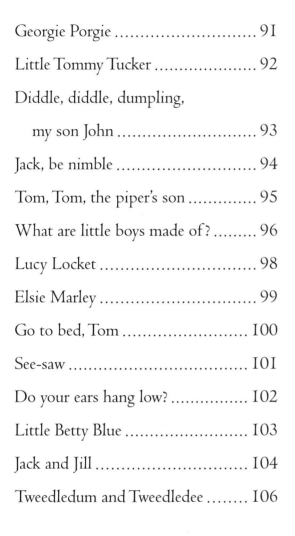

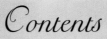

Contents

A Merry Old Soul

OLD KING COLE

Old King Cole
   Was a merry old soul,
And a merry old soul was he.
He called for his pipe,
And he called for his bowl,
And he called for his fiddlers three.
Every fiddler, he had a fiddle,
And a very fine fiddle had he;
Twee tweedle dee, tweedle dee,
   went the fiddlers.
Oh, there's none so rare,
As can compare
With King Cole and
   his fiddlers three.

HANDY SPANDY

Handy Spandy, Jack-a-dandy,
Loves plum cake and sugar candy.
He bought some at the grocer's shop,
And out he came, hop, hop, hop!

HUMPTY DUMPTY

Humpty Dumpty sat on a wall,
Humpty Dumpty had a great fall;
All the king's horses and all the king's men
Couldn't put Humpty together again.

THERE WAS AN OLD WOMAN
WHO LIVED IN A SHOE

There was an old woman
   Who lived in a shoe,
She had so many children
She didn't know what to do;
She gave them some broth
Without any bread;
She scolded them soundly
And put them to bed.

THE MUFFIN MAN

Oh, do you know the muffin man,
The muffin man, the muffin man?
Oh, do you know the muffin man
That lives in Drury Lane?

Oh, yes, I know the muffin man,
The muffin man, the muffin man.
Oh, yes, I know the muffin man
That lives in Drury Lane.

WEE WILLIE WINKIE

Wee Willie Winkie runs through the town,
Upstairs and downstairs in his nightgown,
Rapping at the window, crying through the lock,
'Are all the children in their beds,
It's past eight o'clock!'

THERE WAS A CROOKED MAN

There was a crooked man, and he went a crooked mile,
He found a crooked sixpence against a crooked stile:
He bought a crooked cat, which caught a crooked mouse,
And they all lived together in a little crooked house.

THE GRAND OLD DUKE OF YORK

Oh, the grand old Duke of York,
He had ten thousand men;
He marched them up to the top of the hill,
And he marched them down again.
And when they were up, they were up,
And when they were down, they were down;
And when they were only halfway up,
They were neither up nor down.

THE HOUSE THAT JACK BUILT

This is the house that Jack built.

This is the malt,
That lay in the house that Jack built.

This is the rat,
That ate the malt,
That lay in the house that Jack built.

This is the cat,
That killed the rat,
That ate the malt,
That lay in the house that Jack built.

This is the dog,
That worried the cat,
That killed the rat,
That ate the malt,
That lay in the house that Jack built.

This is the cow with the crumpled horn,
That tossed the dog,
That worried the cat,
That killed the rat,
That ate the malt,
That lay in the house that Jack built.

This is the maiden all forlorn,
That milked the cow with the crumpled horn,
That tossed the dog,
That worried the cat,
That killed the rat,
That ate the malt,
That lay in the house that Jack built.

This is the man all tattered and torn,
That kissed the maiden all forlorn,
That milked the cow with the crumpled horn,
That tossed the dog,
That worried the cat,
That killed the rat,
That ate the malt,
That lay in the house that Jack built.

This is the priest all shaven and shorn,
That married the man all tattered and torn,
That kissed the maiden all forlorn,
That milked the cow with the crumpled horn,
That tossed the dog,
That worried the cat,
That killed the rat,
That ate the malt,
That lay in the house that Jack built.

This is the cock that crowed in the morn,
That waked the priest all shaven and shorn,
That married the man all tattered and torn,
That kissed the maiden all forlorn,
That milked the cow with the crumpled horn,
That tossed the dog,
That worried the cat,
That killed the rat,
That ate the malt,
That lay in the house that Jack built.

This is the farmer sowing his corn,
That kept the cock that crowed in the morn,
That waked the priest all shaven and shorn,
That married the man all tattered and torn,
That kissed the maiden all forlorn,
That milked the cow with the crumpled horn,
That tossed the dog,
That worried the cat,
That killed the rat,
That ate the malt,
That lay in the house that Jack built.

YANKEE DOODLE

Yankee Doodle came to town,
Riding on a pony;
He stuck a feather in his cap
And called it macaroni.

PETER, PETER, PUMPKIN EATER

Peter, Peter, pumpkin eater,
    Had a wife and couldn't keep her;
He put her in a pumpkin shell
And there he kept her very well.

Peter, Peter, pumpkin eater,
Had another and didn't love her;
Peter learned to read and spell,
And then he loved her very well.

COBBLER, COBBLER

Cobbler, cobbler, mend my shoe,
Have it done by half past two.
Half past two is much too late!
Have it done by half past eight.

SIMPLE SIMON

Simple Simon met a pieman,
  Going to the fair;
Said Simple Simon to the pieman,
'Let me taste your ware.'

Said the pieman to Simple Simon,
'Show me first your penny';
Said Simple Simon to the pieman,
'Indeed, I have not any.'

Simple Simon went a-fishing,
For to catch a whale;
All the water he had got
Was in his mother's pail.

Simple Simon went to look
If plums grew on a thistle;
He pricked his fingers very much,
Which made poor Simon whistle.

He went for water in a sieve
But soon it all fell through;
And now poor Simple Simon
Bids you all adieu.

COCK A DOODLE DOO

Cock a doodle doo!
My dame has lost her shoe;
My master's lost his fiddling-stick,
And doesn't know what to do.

Cock a doodle doo!
What is my dame to do?
Till master finds his fiddling-stick,
She'll dance without her shoe.

Cock a doodle doo!
My dame has found her shoe,
And master's found his
 fiddling-stick,
Sing doodle doodle doo!

Cock a doodle doo!
My dame will dance with you,
While master fiddles his
 fiddling-stick,
For dame and doodle doo.

Cock a doodle doo!
Dame has lost her shoe;
Gone to bed and scratched her head
And can't tell what to do.

GREGORY GRIGGS

Gregory Griggs, Gregory Griggs,
  Had twenty-seven different wigs.
He wore them up, he wore them down,
To please the people of the town.
He wore them east, he wore them west,
But he never could tell which he loved best.

And On That Farm

OLD McDONALD HAD A FARM

Old McDonald had a farm,
E-I-E-I-O!
And on that farm he had a cow,
E-I-E-I-O!
With a moo-moo here, and a moo-moo there,
Here a moo, there a moo,
Everywhere a moo-moo!
Old McDonald had a farm,
E-I-E-I-O!

Old McDonald had a farm,
E-I-E-I-O!
And on that farm he had a pig,
E-I-E-I-O!
With an oink-oink here, and an oink-oink there,
Here an oink, there an oink,
Everywhere an oink-oink!
Old McDonald had a farm,
E-I-E-I-O!

Old McDonald had a farm,
E-I-E-I-O!
And on that farm he had a horse,
E-I-E-I-O!
With a neigh-neigh here, and a neigh-neigh there,
Here a neigh, there a neigh,
Everywhere a neigh-neigh!
Old McDonald had a farm,
E-I-E-I-O!

Old McDonald had a farm,
E-I-E-I-O!
And on that farm he had some sheep,
E-I-E-I-O!
With a baa-baa here, and a baa-baa there,
Here a baa, there a baa,
Everywhere a baa-baa!
Old McDonald had a farm,
E-I-E-I-O!

Old McDonald had a farm,
E-I-E-I-O!
And on that farm he had a duck,
E-I-E-I-O!
With a quack-quack here,
and a quack-quack there,
Here a quack, there a quack,
Everywhere a quack-quack!
Old McDonald had a farm,
E-I-E-I-O!

Old McDonald had a farm,
E-I-E-I-O!
And on that farm he had a dog,
E-I-E-I-O!
With a woof-woof here, and a woof-woof there,
Here a woof, there a woof,
Everywhere a woof-woof!
Old McDonald had a farm,
E-I-E-I-O!

HICKETY, PICKETY

Hickety, pickety, my black hen,
    She lays eggs for gentlemen;
Gentlemen come every day
To see what my black hen doth lay;
Sometimes nine and sometimes ten,
Hickety, pickety, my black hen.

GOOSEY, GOOSEY GANDER

Goosey, goosey gander,
    Whither shall I wander?
Upstairs and downstairs
And in my lady's chamber;
There I met an old man
Who would not say his prayers;
I took him by the left leg
And threw him down the stairs.

HIGGLETY, PIGGLETY, POP!

Higglety, pigglety, pop!
The dog has eaten the mop;
The pig's in a hurry,
The cat's in a flurry,
Higglety, pigglety, pop!

I HAD A LITTLE HEN

I had a little hen,
    The prettiest ever seen;
She washed up the dishes,
And kept the house clean.
She went to the mill
To fetch me some flour,
She brought it home
In less than an hour.
She baked me my bread,
She brewed me my ale,
She sat by the fire
And told many a fine tale.

FLOUR

LITTLE BO-PEEP

*L*ittle Bo-Peep has lost her sheep,
  And can't tell where to find them;
Leave them alone, and they'll come home,
And bring their tails behind them.

Little Bo-Peep fell fast asleep,
And dreamed she heard them bleating;
But when she awoke she found it a joke,
For they were still a-fleeting.

Then up she took her little crook,
Determined for to find them;
She found them indeed, but it made her heart bleed,
For they'd left their tails behind them.

It happened one day, as Bo-Peep did stray
Into a meadow hard by,
There she spied their tails side by side,
All hung on a tree to dry.

She heaved a sigh, and wiped her eye,
And over the hillocks went rambling,
And tried what she could, as a shepherdess should,
To tack each again to its lambkin.

MARY HAD A LITTLE LAMB

Mary had a little lamb,
Its fleece was white as snow;
And everywhere that Mary went
The lamb was sure to go.

It followed her to school one day,
Which was against the rule;
It made the children laugh and play
To see a lamb at school.

And so the teacher turned it out,
But still it lingered near,
And waited patiently about
Till Mary did appear.

'What makes the lamb love Mary so?'
The eager children cry;
'Why, Mary loves the lamb, you know,'
The teacher did reply.

To market, to market

To market, to market, to buy a fat pig,
Home again, home again, jiggety-jig;
To market, to market, to buy a fat hog,
Home again, home again, jiggety-jog.
To market, to market, to buy a plum bun;
Home again, home again, market is done.

THREE BLIND MICE

Three blind mice, see how they run!
They all ran after the farmer's wife,
Who cut off their tails with a carving knife;
Did you ever see such a thing in your life,
As three blind mice?

I ASKED MY MOTHER FOR FIFTY CENTS

I asked my mother for fifty cents,
　　To see the elephant jump the fence,
He jumped so high,
He reached the sky,
And didn't come back till the fourth of July.

BAA, BAA, BLACK SHEEP

Baa, baa, black sheep,
Have you any wool?
Yes, sir, yes, sir,
Three bags full;
One for the master,
And one for the dame,
And one for the little boy
Who lives down the lane.

Mother Goose

Old Mother Goose,
    When she wanted to wander,
Would ride through the air
On a very fine gander.

Mother Goose had a house,
'Twas built in a wood,
Where an owl at the door
For a sentinel stood.

She had a son Jack,
A plain-looking lad,
He was not very good,
Nor yet very bad.

She sent him to market,
A live goose he bought:
'See, Mother,' says he,
'I have not been for naught.'

Jack's goose and her gander
Grew very fond;
They'd both eat together,
Or swim in the pond.

Jack found one morning,
As I have been told,
His goose had laid him
An egg of pure gold.

Jack rode to his mother,
The news for to tell.
She called him a good boy,
And said it was well.

Jack sold his gold egg
To a merchant untrue,
Who cheated him out of
A half of his due.

Then Jack went a-courting
A lady so gay,
As fair as the lily,
And sweet as the May.

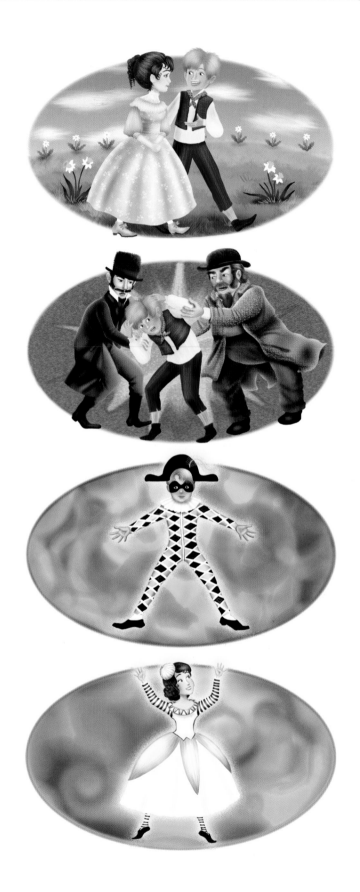

The merchant and squire
Soon came at his back
And began to belabour
The sides of poor Jack.

Then old Mother Goose
That instant came in,
And turned her son Jack
Into famed Harlequin.

She then, with her wand,
Touched the lady so fine,
And turned her at once
Into sweet Columbine.

The gold egg in the sea
Was thrown away then,
When an odd fish brought her
The egg back again.

The merchant then vowed
The goose he would kill
Resolving at once
His pockets to fill.

Jack's mother came in,
And caught the goose soon,
And mounting its back,
Flew up to the moon.

MONKEYS ON THE BED

Three little monkeys
    Jumping on the bed;
One fell off
And knocked his head.
Momma called the doctor,
The doctor said:
'No more monkeys
    Jumping on the bed.'

SIX LITTLE MICE

Six little mice sat down to spin,
   Pussy passed by, and she peeped in.
What are you doing, my little men?
Weaving coats for gentlemen.
Shall I come in and cut off your threads?
No, no, Mistress Pussy, you'd bite off our heads!
Oh, no, I won't, I'll help you to spin.
That may be so, but you can't come in!

A WISE OLD OWL

A wise old owl lived in an oak,
The more he saw the less he spoke;
The less he spoke the more he heard.
Why aren't we all like that wise old bird?

POP GOES THE WEASEL!

Up and down the City Road,
In and out the Eagle,
That's the way the money goes,
Pop goes the weasel!

Half a pound of tuppenny rice,
Half a pound of treacle,
Mix it up and make it nice,
Pop goes the weasel!

Every night when I go out
The monkey's on the table,
Take a stick and knock it off,
Pop goes the weasel!

Hey, diddle, diddle

Hey, diddle, diddle, the cat and the fiddle,
The cow jumped over the moon;
The little dog laughed to see such sport,
And the dish ran away with the spoon.

GREY GOOSE AND GANDER

Grey goose and gander
  Waft your wings together,
And carry the good king's daughter
Over the one-strand river.

RIDE A COCK-HORSE

Ride a cock-horse to Banbury Cross,
To see a fine lady upon a white horse;
With rings on her fingers and bells on her toes,
She shall have music wherever she goes.

FUZZY WUZZY

Fuzzy Wuzzy was a bear,
A bear was Fuzzy Wuzzy.
When Fuzzy Wuzzy lost his hair
He wasn't fuzzy, was he?

We'll All Have Tea

POLLY PUT THE KETTLE ON

Polly, put the kettle on,
  Polly, put the kettle on,
Polly, put the kettle on,
We'll all have tea.

Sukey, take it off again,
Sukey, take it off again,
Sukey, take it off again,
They've all gone away.

LITTLE JACK HORNER

Little Jack Horner
Sat in a corner,
Eating a Christmas pie;
He put in his thumb,
And pulled out a plum,
And said, 'What a
good boy am I!'

SING A SONG OF SIXPENCE

Sing a song of sixpence,
A pocket full of rye;
Four and twenty blackbirds
Baked in a pie.

When the pie was opened
The birds began to sing;
Wasn't that a dainty dish
To set before the king?

The king was in his counting-house
Counting out his money;
The queen was in the parlour
Eating bread and honey.

The maid was in the garden
Hanging out the clothes,
When down came a blackbird,
And pecked off her nose.

RYE

A WAS AN APPLE PIE

A was an apple pie

B bit it

C cut it

D dealt it

E eat it

F fought for it

G got it

H had it

I inspected it

J jumped for it

K kept it

L longed for it

M mourned it

N nodded at it

O opened it

P peeped in it

Q quartered it

R ran for it

S stole it

T took it

U upset it

V viewed it

W wanted it

X, Y, Z and ampersand

All wished for a piece in hand.

Hot cross buns!

Hot cross buns!
Hot cross buns!
One a penny, two a penny,
Hot cross buns!

If you have no daughters,
Give them to your sons.
One a penny, two a penny,
Hot cross buns!

BETTY BOTTER

Betty Botter bought some butter,
But, she said, the butter's bitter;
If I put it in my batter
It will make my batter bitter,
But a bit of better butter
That would make my batter better.
So she bought a bit of butter
Better than her bitter butter,
And she put it in her batter
And the batter was not bitter.
So 'twas better Betty Botter
Bought a bit of better butter.

JACK SPRAT

Jack Sprat could eat no fat,
His wife could eat no lean,
And so between them both, you see,
They licked the platter clean.

PEASE PORRIDGE HOT

Pease porridge hot,
   Pease porridge cold,
Pease porridge in the pot,
Nine days old.

Some like it hot,
Some like it cold,
Some like it in the pot,
Nine days old.

THE QUEEN OF HEARTS

The Queen of Hearts,
She made some tarts,
All on a summer's day;
The Knave of Hearts,
He stole those tarts,
And took them clean away.

The King of Hearts,
Called for the tarts,
And beat the Knave full sore;
The Knave of Hearts
Brought back the tarts,
And vowed he'd steal no more.

PETER PIPER

Peter Piper picked a peck of pickled peppers;
   A peck of pickled peppers Peter Piper picked;
If Peter Piper picked a peck of pickled peppers,
Where's the peck of pickled peppers Peter Piper picked?

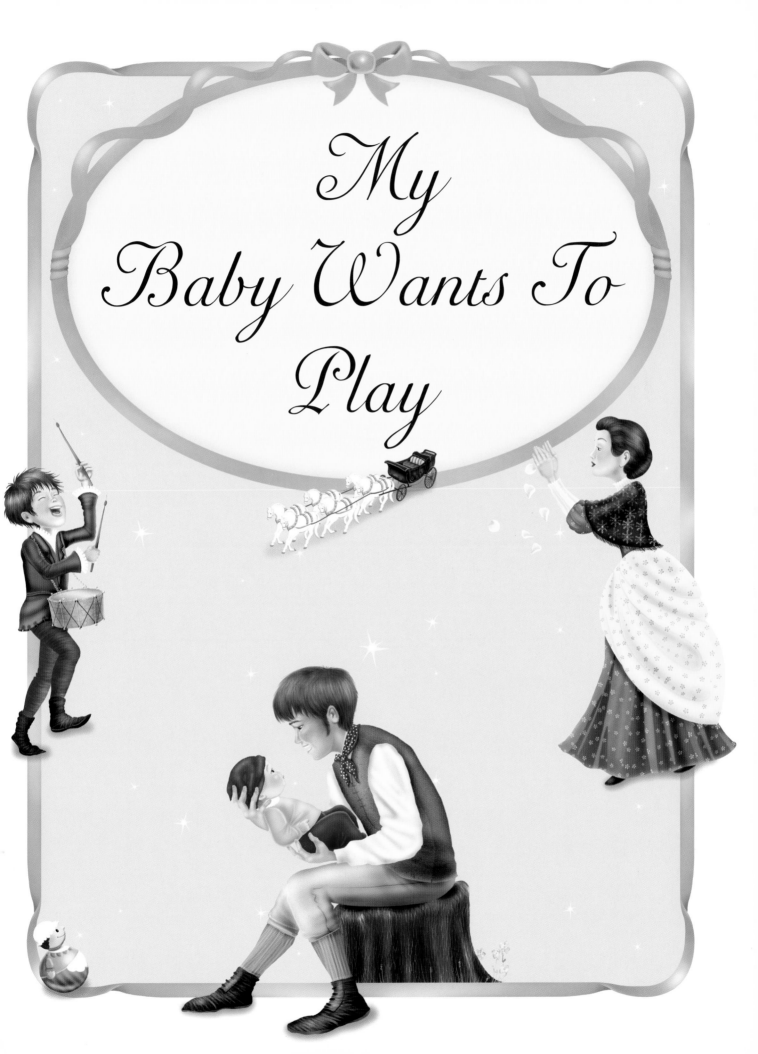

My
Baby Wants To
Play

HOW MANY DAYS HAS MY BABY TO PLAY?

How many days has my baby to play?
Saturday, Sunday, Monday,
Tuesday, Wednesday, Thursday, Friday,
Saturday, Sunday, Monday.
Hop away, skip away,
My baby wants to play,
My baby wants to play every day!

ROCK-A-BYE, BABY, ON THE TREE TOP

Rock-a-bye, baby, on the tree top,
When the wind blows, the cradle will rock;
When the bough breaks, the cradle will fall,
Down will come baby, cradle and all.

HUSH, LITTLE BABY

Hush, little baby, don't say a word,
Papa's going to buy you a mocking bird.

If that mocking bird won't sing,
Papa's going to buy you a diamond ring.

If that diamond ring turns brass,
Papa's going to buy you a looking glass.

If that looking glass gets broke,
Papa's going to buy you a billy goat.

If that billy goat won't pull,
Papa's going to buy you a cart and bull.

If that cart and bull turn over,
Papa's going to buy you a dog named Rover.

If that dog named Rover won't bark,
Papa's going to buy you a horse and cart.

If that horse and cart fall down,
You'll still be the sweetest little baby in town.

SLEEP, BABY, SLEEP

Sleep, baby, sleep,
   Thy father guards the sheep,
Thy mother shakes the dreamland tree,
And from it fall sweet dreams for thee.
Sleep, baby, sleep.

Sleep, baby, sleep,
Our cottage vale is deep.
The little lamb is on the green,
With woolly fleece so soft and clean.
Sleep, baby, sleep.

Sleep, baby, sleep,
Down where the woodbines creep.
Be always like the lamb so mild,
A kind and sweet and gentle child.
Sleep, baby, sleep.

BYE, BABY BUNTING

Bye, baby bunting,
Daddy's gone a-hunting,
To fetch a little rabbit skin
To wrap his baby bunting in.

ALL THE PRETTY LITTLE HORSES

Hush-a-bye, don't you cry
Go to sleep, little baby.
When you wake
You shall have
All the pretty little horses,
Blacks and bays,
Dapples and greys,
Coach and six white horses.

Hush-a-bye, don't you cry,
Go to sleep, little baby.
When you wake
You shall have cake
And all the pretty little horses.

COME TO THE WINDOW

Come to the window,
My baby, with me,
And look at the stars
That shine on the sea!
There are two little stars
That play at bo-peep
With two little fishes
Far down in the deep.
And two little frogs
Cry, 'Neap, neap, neap,
I see a dear baby
That should be asleep!'

ROCK-A-BYE, BABY, THY CRADLE IS GREEN

Rock-a-bye, baby, thy cradle is green,
Father's a nobleman, Mother's a queen.
And Betty's a lady and wears a gold ring,
And Johnny's a drummer and drums for the king.

MOSES SUPPOSES

Moses supposes his toes are roses,
But Moses supposes erroneously.

For Moses he knows his toes aren't roses,
As Moses supposes his toes to be!

How Does Your Garden Grow?

MARY, MARY, QUITE CONTRARY

Mary, Mary, quite contrary,
How does your garden grow?
With silver bells and cockle shells,
And pretty maids all in a row.

HERE WE GO ROUND THE MULBERRY BUSH

Here we go round the mulberry bush,
The mulberry bush, the mulberry bush.
Here we go round the mulberry bush,
On a cold and frosty morning.

This is the way we wash our clothes,
Wash our clothes, wash our clothes.
This is the way we wash our clothes,
On a cold and frosty morning.

IT'S RAINING, IT'S POURING

It's raining, it's pouring,
 The old man is snoring;
He went to bed and bumped his head
And couldn't get up in the morning.

SHE SELLS SEA-SHELLS ON THE SEA SHORE

She sells sea-shells on the sea shore,
  The shells that she sells are sea-shells, I'm sure.
So if she sells sea-shells on the sea shore,
I'm sure that the shells are sea-shore shells.

RAIN, RAIN, GO AWAY

Rain, rain, go away,
Come again another day.
Little Johnny wants to play.

Come With
A Whoop

GIRLS AND BOYS, COME OUT TO PLAY

Girls and boys, come out to play,
   The moon doth shine as bright as day.
Leave your supper and leave your sleep,
And join your playfellows into the street.
Come with a whoop and come with a call,
Come with a good will or not at all.
Up the ladder and down the wall,
A half-penny loaf will serve us all;
You find milk and I'll find flour,
And we'll have a pudding in half an hour.

LITTLE BOY BLUE

Little Boy Blue,
Come blow your horn,
The sheep's in the meadow,
The cow's in the corn.

Where is the boy
Who looks after the sheep?
He's under the haystack,
Fast asleep.

Will you wake him?
No, not I,
For if I do,
He's sure to cry.

THERE WAS A LITTLE GIRL

There was a little girl, and she had a little curl
  Right in the middle of her forehead;
When she was good, she was very, very good,
But when she was bad, she was horrid.

SALLY, GO ROUND THE SUN

Sally, go round the sun,
Sally, go round the moon,
Sally, go round the chimneypots,
On a Saturday afternoon.

GEORGIE PORGIE

Georgie Porgie, pudding and pie,
  Kissed the girls and made them cry;
When the boys came out to play,
Georgie Porgie ran away.

LITTLE TOMMY TUCKER

Little Tommy Tucker
Sings for his supper;
What shall he eat?
Brown bread and butter.
How shall he cut it
Without e'er a knife?
How will he be married
Without e'er a wife?

DIDDLE, DIDDLE, DUMPLING, MY SON JOHN

Diddle, diddle, dumpling, my son John,
    Went to bed with his trousers on;
One shoe off, and one shoe on,
Diddle, diddle, dumpling, my son John.

JACK, BE NIMBLE

Jack, be nimble,
Jack, be quick,
Jack, jump over
The candlestick.

TOM, TOM, THE PIPER'S SON

Tom, Tom, the piper's son
    Stole a pig and away did run;
The pig was eat
And Tom was beat,
And Tom went howling down the street.

WHAT ARE LITTLE BOYS MADE OF?

What are little boys made of, made of?
What are little boys made of?
Frogs and snails and puppy dogs' tails,
That's what little boys are made of.

What are little girls made of, made of?
What are little girls made of?
Sugar and spice and all things nice,
That's what little girls are made of.

PUPPY
DOGS' TAILS

Spice

SUGAR

SPICE

LUCY LOCKET

Lucy Locket lost her pocket,
Kitty Fisher found it.
Not a penny was there in it
But a ribbon round it.

ELSIE MARLEY

Elsie Marley is grown so fine,
She won't get up to feed the swine,
But lies in bed till eight or nine,
And surely she does take her time.

GO TO BED, TOM

Go to bed, Tom,
Go to bed, Tom,
Tired or not, Tom,
Go to bed, Tom.

SEE-SAW

See-saw, Margery Daw,
  Jacky shall have a new master;
He shall have but a penny a day,
Because he can't work any faster.

Do your ears hang low?

Do your ears hang low?
  Do they wobble to and fro?
Can you tie them in a knot?
Can you tie them in a bow?
Can you throw them over your shoulder,
Like a regimental soldier?
Do your ears hang low?

LITTLE BETTY BLUE

Little Betty Blue
Lost her holiday shoe.
What can little Betty do?
Give her another
To match the other,
And then she may walk in two.

JACK AND JILL

Jack and Jill went up the hill
　　To fetch a pail of water;
　　Jack fell down and broke his crown,
And Jill came tumbling after.

Then up Jack got and home did trot
As fast as he could caper;
He went to bed to mend his head
With vinegar and brown paper.

TWEEDLEDUM AND TWEEDLEDEE

Tweedledum and Tweedledee
  Agreed to fight a battle,
For Tweedledum said Tweedledee
Had spoilt his nice new rattle.
Just then flew by a monstrous crow
As big as a tar barrel,
Which frightened both the heroes so,
They quite forgot their quarrel.

Wriggle Your Hips

NUMBER ONE, TICKLE YOUR TUM

*N*umber one, tickle your tum,

Number two, just say 'Boo!'

Number three, touch your knee,

Number four, touch the floor,

Number five, do a dive,

Number six, wriggle your hips,

Number seven, jump to heaven,

Number eight, stand up straight,

Number nine, walk in a line,

Number ten, do it all again!

RING-A-RING O' ROSES

Ring-a-ring o' roses
A pocket full of posies,
A-tishoo! A-tishoo!
We all fall down.

The cows are in the meadow,
Lying fast asleep.
A-tishoo! A-tishoo!
We all get up again.

ROUND AND ROUND THE GARDEN

Round and round the garden,
Like a teddy bear.
One step, two steps,
Tickle you under there!

THIS LITTLE PIGGY

This little piggy went to market,
This little piggy stayed at home;
This little piggy had roast beef,
This little piggy had none;
And this little piggy cried,
'Wee-wee-wee,'
All the way home.

INCY WINCY SPIDER

Incy Wincy Spider
  Climbed up the water spout.
Down came the rain
And washed poor Incy out.

Out came the sunshine
And dried up all the rain,
And Incy Wincy Spider
Climbed up the spout again.

ORANGES AND LEMONS

'Oranges and lemons,'
    Say the bells of St Clements.

'You owe me five farthings,'
Say the bells of St Martins.

'When will you pay me?'
Say the bells of Old Bailey.

'When I grow rich,'
Say the bells at Shoreditch.

'When will that be?'
Say the bells of Stepney.

'I'm sure I don't know,'
Says the great bell at Bow.

Here comes the candle to light you to bed,
Here comes the chopper to chop off your head,
Chip chop, chip chop, the last man's head!

I'm a Little Teapot

I'm a little teapot, short and stout,
    Here is my handle, here is my spout.
When I see the teacups, then I shout,
'Tip me over and pour me out.'

HERE IS THE CHURCH

Here is the church,
And here's the steeple,
Open the doors,
And see all the people.

TWINKLE, TWINKLE, LITTLE STAR

Twinkle, twinkle, little star,
How I wonder what you are!
Up above the world so high,
Like a diamond in the sky.

When the blazing sun is gone,
When he nothing shines upon,
Then you show your little light,
Twinkle, twinkle all the night.

Then the traveller in the dark,
Thanks you for your tiny spark,
He could not see which way to go,
If you did not twinkle so.

In the dark blue sky you keep,
And often through my curtains peep,
Do you never shut your eye
Till the sun is in the sky.

As your bright and tiny spark
Lights the traveller in the dark,
Though I know not what you are,
Twinkle, twinkle little star.

TEDDY BEAR, TEDDY BEAR

Teddy bear, teddy bear,
Turn around.

Teddy bear, teddy bear,
Touch the ground.

Teddy bear, teddy bear,
Climb the stairs.

Teddy bear, teddy bear,
Say your prayers.

Teddy bear, teddy bear,
Turn out the light.

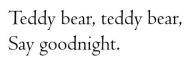

Teddy bear, teddy bear,
Say goodnight.

PAT-A-CAKE

Pat-a-cake, pat-a-cake, baker's man,
Bake me a cake as fast as you can;
Pat it and prick it and mark it with B,
Put it in the oven for Baby and me.

The Dog Made A Bow

OLD MOTHER HUBBARD

*O*ld Mother Hubbard
Went to the cupboard
To fetch her poor dog a bone;
But when she got there,
The cupboard was bare,
And so the poor dog had none.

She went to the baker's
To buy him some bread;
But when she came back
The poor dog was dead.

She went to the undertaker's
To buy him a coffin;
But when she came back
The poor dog was laughing.

She went to the fishmonger's
To buy him some fish;
But when she came back
He was washing the dish.

She went to the tavern
For white wine and red;
But when she came back
The dog stood on his head.

She went to the hatter's
To buy him a hat;
But when she came back
He was feeding the cat.

She went to the barber's
To buy him a wig;
But when she came back,
He was dancing a jig.

She went to the fruiterer's
To buy him some fruit;
But when she came back,
He was playing the flute.

She went to the tailor's
To buy him a coat;
But when she came back
He was riding a goat.

She went to the cobbler's
To buy him some shoes,
But when she came back
He was reading the news.

She went to the seamstress
To buy him some linen;
But when she came back
The dog was a-spinning.

She went to the hosier's
To buy him some hose;
But when she came back
He was dressed in his clothes.

The dame made a curtsy,
The dog made a bow;
The dame said, 'Your servant!'
The dog said, 'Bow-wow.'

HICKORY, DICKORY, DOCK

Hickory, dickory, dock,
The mouse ran up the clock,
The clock struck one,
The mouse ran down,
Hickory, dickory, dock.

Oh where, oh where, has my little dog gone?

Oh where, oh where,
 Has my little dog gone?
Oh where, oh where can he be?

With his ears cut short
And his tail cut long,
Oh where, oh where is he?

THREE LITTLE KITTENS

Three little kittens, they lost their mittens,
And they began to cry;
Oh, mother dear, we sadly fear
That we have lost our mittens.
What! Lost your mittens, you naughty kittens!
Then you shall have no pie.
Mee-ow, mee-ow, mee-ow,
No, you shall have no pie.

Three little kittens, they found their mittens,
And they began to cry;
Oh, mother dear, see here, see here,
For we have found our mittens.
Put on your mittens, you silly kittens,
And you shall have some pie.
Purr-r, purr-r, purr-r,
Oh, let us have some pie.

Three little kittens put on their mittens,
And soon ate up the pie;
Oh, mother dear, we greatly fear
That we have soiled our mittens.
What! Soiled your mittens, you naughty kittens!
Then they began to sigh,
Mee-ow, mee-ow, mee-ow,
Then they began to sigh.

The three little kittens, they washed their mittens,
And hung them out to dry;
Oh, mother dear, do you not hear
That we have washed our mittens?
What! Washed your mittens, you good little kittens,
But I smell a rat close by.
Mee-ow, mee-ow, mee-ow,
We smell a rat close by.

DING DONG BELL

Ding dong bell,
Pussy's in the well.
Who put her in?
Little Johnny Green.
Who pulled her out?
Little Tommy Stout.
What a naughty boy was that,
To try to drown poor pussy cat,
Who never did him any harm,
But killed the mice in his father's barn.

LITTLE MISS MUFFET

Little Miss Muffet
   Sat on a tuffet,
Eating her curds and whey;
Along came a spider,
Who sat down beside her
And frightened
   Miss Muffet away.

THE NORTH WIND DOTH BLOW

The north wind doth blow,
And we shall have snow,
And what will poor Robin do then,
Poor thing?

He'll sit in a barn,
And keep himself warm,
And hide his head under his wing,
Poor thing.

The north wind doth blow,
And we shall have snow,
And what shall the honey-bee do,
Poor thing?

In his hive he will stay,
Till the cold's passed away,
And then he'll come out in the spring,
Poor thing.

The north wind doth blow,
And we shall have snow,
And what will the dormouse do then,
Poor thing?

Rolled up like a ball,
In his nest snug and small,
He'll sleep till warm weather comes back,
Poor thing.

The north wind doth blow,
And we shall have snow,
And what will the children do then,
Poor things?

When lessons are done,
They'll jump, skip and run,
And that's how they'll keep themselves warm,
Poor things.

TWO CATS OF KILKENNY

There once were two cats of Kilkenny,
  Each thought there was one cat too many.
So they fought and they fit,
And they scratched and they bit,
Till, excepting their nails,
And the tips of their tails,
Instead of two cats, there weren't any.

The One You Love The Best

LITTLE SALLY WATERS

Little Sally Waters,
Sitting in the sun,
Crying and weeping,
For a young man.
Rise, Sally, rise,
Dry your weeping eyes,
Fly to the east,
Fly to the west,
Fly to the one you love the best.

CURLY LOCKS

Curly Locks! Curly Locks! Will you be mine?
You shall not wash dishes, nor yet feed the swine,
But sit on a cushion and sew a fine seam,
And feed upon strawberries, sugar and cream.

A Froggie went a-courtin'

A Froggie went a-courtin' and he did ride;
Sword and pistol by his side.

He rode to Miss Mousie's hall,
Gave a loud knock and gave a loud call.

'Pray, Miss Mousie, are you within?'
'Yes, kind sir, I sit and spin.'

He took Miss Mousie on his knee,
And said, 'Miss Mousie, will you marry me?'

Miss Mousie blushed and hung her head,
'You'll have to ask Uncle Rat,' she said.

'Not without Uncle Rat's consent
Would I marry the President.'

Uncle Rat jumped up and shook his fat side,
To think his niece would be Bill Frog's bride.

Next day Uncle Rat went to town,
To buy his niece a wedding gown.

Where shall the wedding supper be?
Way down yonder in a hollow tree.

First to come in was a bumblebee,
Who played the fiddle on his knee.

The next to come was Captain Flea,
Danced a jig with the bumblebee.

Then Froggie and Mouse went off to France,
And that's the end of my romance.

THE OWL AND THE PUSSYCAT

The Owl and the Pussycat went to sea
  In a beautiful pea-green boat;
They took some honey, and plenty of money
Wrapped up in a five-pound note.
The Owl looked up to the stars above,
And sang to a small guitar,
'O lovely Pussy, O Pussy, my love,
What a beautiful Pussy you are,
You are, you are!
What a beautiful pussy you are!'

Pussy said to the Owl, 'You elegant fowl,
How charmingly sweet you sing!
O, let us be married; too long have we tarried:
But what shall we do for a ring?'
They sailed away, for a year and a day,
To the land where the bong-tree grows,
And there in a wood a Piggy-wig stood,
With a ring at the end of his nose,
His nose, his nose,
With a ring at the end of his nose.

'Dear Pig, are you willing to sell for one shilling
Your ring?' Said the Piggy, 'I will.'
So they took it away, and were married next day
By the turkey who lives on the hill.
They dined on mince and slices of quince,
Which they ate with a runcible spoon;
And hand in hand, on the edge of the sand,
They danced by the light of the moon,
The moon, the moon,
They danced by the light of the moon.

Edward Lear

A TISKET, A TASKET

A tisket, a tasket,
A green and yellow basket.
I wrote a letter to my love,
But on the way I dropped it.
I dropped it, I dropped it,
And on the way, I dropped it.
A little boy picked it up,
And put it in his pocket.

Seven
For A Secret

ONE FOR SORROW, TWO FOR JOY

One for sorrow, two for joy,
Three for a girl and four for a boy,
Five for silver, six for gold,
Seven for a secret never to be told,
Eight for a letter over the sea,
Nine for a lover as true as can be.

One, Two, Buckle My Shoe

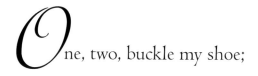

One, two, buckle my shoe;

Three, four, knock on the door;

Five, six, pick up sticks;

Seven, eight, lay them straight;

Nine, ten, a good fat hen.

Eleven, twelve, dig and delve;

Thirteen, fourteen, maids a-courting;

Fifteen, sixteen, maids in the kitchen;

Seventeen, eighteen, maids a-waiting;

Nineteen, twenty, my plate's empty.

THERE WERE TEN IN THE BED

There were ten in the bed
    And the little one said,
'Roll over! Roll over!'
So they all rolled over
And one fell out,
And he gave a little scream,
And he gave a little shout, 'Yahoo!'
Please remember to tie a knot in
    your pyjamas,
Single beds are only made for
One, two, three, four, five, six, seven, eight –

There were nine in the bed
And the little one said,
'Roll over! Roll over!'
So they all rolled over
And one fell out,
And he gave a little scream,
And he gave a little shout, 'Yahoo!'
Please remember to tie a knot in your pyjamas,
Single beds are only made for
One, two, three, four, five, six, seven –

There were eight in the bed
And the little one said,
'Roll over! Roll over!'
So they all rolled over
And one fell out,
And he gave a little scream,
And he gave a little shout, 'Yahoo!'
Please remember to tie a knot in your pyjamas,
Single beds are only made for
One, two, three, four, five, six –

There were seven in the bed
And the little one said,
'Roll over! Roll over!'
So they all rolled over
And one fell out,
And he gave a little scream,
And he gave a little shout, 'Yahoo!'
Please remember to tie a knot in
    your pyjamas,
Single beds are only made for
One, two, three, four, five –

There were six in the bed
And the little one said,
'Roll over! Roll over!'
So they all rolled over
And one fell out,
And he gave a little scream,
And he gave a little shout, 'Yahoo!'
Please remember to tie a knot in
      your pyjamas,
Single beds are only made for
One, two, three, four —

There were five in the bed
And the little one said,
'Roll over! Roll over!'
So they all rolled over
And one fell out,
And he gave a little scream,
And he gave a little shout, 'Yahoo!'
Please remember to tie a knot in
    your pyjamas,
Single beds are only made for
One, two, three —

There were four in the bed
And the little one said,
'Roll over! Roll over!'
So they all rolled over
And one fell out,
And he gave a little scream,
And he gave a little shout, 'Yahoo!'
Please remember to tie a knot in
    your pyjamas,
Single beds are only made for
One, two —

There were three in the bed
And the little one said,
'Roll over! Roll over!'
So they all rolled over
And one fell out,
And he gave a little scream,
And he gave a little shout, 'Yahoo!'
Please remember to tie a knot in
    your pyjamas,
Single beds are only made for
One —

There were two in the bed
And the little one said,
'Roll over! Roll over!'
So they all rolled over
And one fell out,
And he gave a little scream,
And he gave a little shout, 'Yahoo!'
Please remember to tie a knot in
   your pyjamas,
Single beds are only made for one.
Single beds are only made for one.

FIVE LITTLE DUCKS

Five little ducks went out one day
   Over the hills and far away.
Mother duck said, 'Quack quack, quack quack!'
But only four little ducks came back.

Four little ducks went out one day
Over the hills and far away.
Mother duck said, 'Quack quack, quack quack!'
But only three little ducks came back.

Three little ducks went out one day
Over the hills and far away.
Mother duck said, 'Quack quack, quack quack!'
But only two little ducks came back.

Two little ducks went out one day
Over the hills and far away.
Mother duck said, 'Quack quack, quack quack!'
But only one little duck came back.

One little duck went out one day
Over the hills and far away.
Mother duck said, 'Quack quack, quack quack!'
But none of those five little ducks came back.

Mother duck she went out one day
Over the hills and far away.
Mother duck said, 'Quack quack, quack quack!'
And all of those five little ducks came back.

THE ANIMALS WENT IN TWO BY TWO

The animals went in two by two,
Hurrah! Hurrah!
The animals went in two by two,
Hurrah! Hurrah!
The animals went in two by two,
The elephant and the kangaroo.
And they all went into the ark
For to get out of the rain.

The animals went in three by three
Hurrah! Hurrah!
The animals went in three by three,
Hurrah! Hurrah!
The animals went in three by three,
The wasp, the ant and the bumblebee.
And they all went into the ark
For to get out of the rain.

The animals went in four by four,
Hurrah! Hurrah!
The animals went in four by four,
Hurrah! Hurrah!

The animals went in four by four,
The great hippopotamus stuck in the door.
And they all went into the ark
For to get out of the rain.

The animals went in five by five,
Hurrah! Hurrah!
The animals went in five by five,
Hurrah! Hurrah!
The animals went in five by five,
They felt so happy to be alive.
And they all went into the ark
For to get out of the rain.

The animals went in six by six,
Hurrah! Hurrah!
The animals went in six by six,
Hurrah! Hurrah!
The animals went in six by six,
They turned out the monkey
    because of his tricks.
And they all went into the ark
For to get out of the rain.

The animals went in seven by seven,
Hurrah! Hurrah!
The animals went in seven by seven,
Hurrah! Hurrah!
The animals went in seven by seven,
The little pig thought he was going
    to heaven.
And they all went into the ark
For to get out of the rain.

The animals went in eight by eight,
Hurrah! Hurrah!
The animals went in eight by eight,
Hurrah! Hurrah!
The animals went in eight by eight,
The slithery snake slid under the gate.
And they all went into the ark
For to get out of the rain.

The animals went in nine by nine,
Hurrah! Hurrah!
The animals went in nine by nine,
Hurrah! Hurrah!

The animals went in nine by nine,
The rhino stood on the porcupine.
And they all went into the ark
For to get out of the rain.

The animals went in ten by ten,
Hurrah! Hurrah!
The animals went in ten by ten,
Hurrah! Hurrah!
The animals went in ten by ten,
And Noah said, 'Let's start again!'
And they all went into the ark
For to get out of the rain.

THREE JELLYFISH

Three jellyfish, three jellyfish,
Three jellyfish, sitting on a rock.
One fell off! … Ooooh … Splash!

Two jellyfish, two jellyfish,
Two jellyfish, sitting on a rock.
One fell off! … Ooooh … Splash!

One jellyfish, one jellyfish,
One jellyfish, sitting on a rock.
One fell off! … Ooooh … Splash!

No jellyfish, no jellyfish,
No jellyfish, sitting on a rock.
One jumped up! … Hooray!

One jellyfish, one jellyfish,
One jellyfish, sitting on a rock.
One jumped up! … Hooray!

Two jellyfish, two jellyfish,
Two jellyfish, sitting on a rock.
One jumped up! … Hooray!

Three jellyfish, three jellyfish,
Three jellyfish, sitting on a rock.
One fell off! … Ooooh … Splash!

THIRTY DAYS HATH SEPTEMBER

Thirty days hath September,
    April, June and November;
February has twenty-eight alone,
All the rest have thirty-one,
Excepting leap-year — that's the time,
When February's days are twenty-nine.

That
Is The Way

SEE, SAW, SACRADOWN

See, saw, sacradown,
　Which is the way to London town?
One foot up, the other foot down,
And that is the way to London town.

THE FLYING PIG

Dickery, dickery, dare,
   The pig flew up in the air;
The man in brown
Soon brought him down.
Dickery, dickery, dare.

I SAW A SHIP A-SAILING

I saw a ship a-sailing,
   A-sailing on the sea;
And oh! It was laden
With pretty things for me.

There were comfits in the cabin,
And apples in the hold;
The sails were made of silk,
And the masts were made of gold.

The four-and-twenty sailors
That stood between the decks,
Were four-and-twenty white mice,
With chains about their necks.

The captain was a duck,
With a packet on his back,
And when the ship began to move,
The captain said, 'Quack, quack!'

As I was going to St Ives

As I was going to St Ives,
I met a man with seven wives.
Each wife had seven sacks.
Each sack had seven cats.
Each cat had seven kits.
Kits, cats, sacks and wives:
How many were going to St Ives?

PUSSYCAT, PUSSYCAT

Pussycat, pussycat, where have you been?
   I've been to London to visit the queen.
Pussycat, pussycat, what did you there?
I frightened a little mouse under her chair.

Row, row, row your boat

Row, row, row your boat,
Gently down the stream,
Merrily, merrily, merrily, merrily,
Life is but a dream.

LONDON BRIDGE

London Bridge is falling down,
Falling down, falling down.
London Bridge is falling down,
My fair lady.

Build it up with sticks and stones,
Sticks and stones, sticks and stones,
Build it up with sticks and stones,
My fair lady.

Sticks and stones will wear away,
Wear away, wear away,
Sticks and stones will wear away,
My fair lady.

Build it up with iron and steel,
Iron and steel, iron and steel,
Build it up with iron and steel,
My fair lady.

Iron and steel will bend and bow,
Bend and bow, bend and bow,
Iron and steel will bend and bow,
My fair lady.

Build it up with bricks and clay,
Bricks and clay, bricks and clay,
Build it up with bricks and clay,
My fair lady.

Bricks and clay will wash away,
Wash away, wash away,
Bricks and clay will wash away,
My fair lady.

Build it up with silver and gold,
Silver and gold, silver and gold,
Build it up with silver and gold,
My fair lady.

Silver and gold will be stole away,
Stole away, stole away,
Silver and gold will be stole away,
My fair lady.

London Bridge is falling down,
Falling down, falling down.
London Bridge is falling down,
My fair lady.

I SAW THREE SHIPS

I saw three ships come sailing by,
    Come sailing by, come sailing by,
I saw three ships come sailing by,
On Christmas Day in the morning.

And what do you think was in them then,
Was in them then, was in them then?
And what do you think was in them then,
On Christmas Day in the morning?

Three pretty girls were in them then,
Were in them then, were in them then,
Three pretty girls were in them then,
On Christmas Day in the morning.

One could whistle, and one could sing,
And one could play on the violin;
So joy there was at my wedding,
On Christmas Day in the morning.

RUB-A-DUB DUB

Rub-a-dub dub,
Three men in a tub,
And who do you think they be?
The butcher, the baker,
The candlestick-maker,
Turn them out, knaves all three.

A SAILOR WENT TO SEA, SEA, SEA

A sailor went to sea, sea, sea,
To see what he could see, see, see;
But all that he could see, see, see,
Was the bottom of the deep blue sea, sea, sea!

Star Light, Star Bright

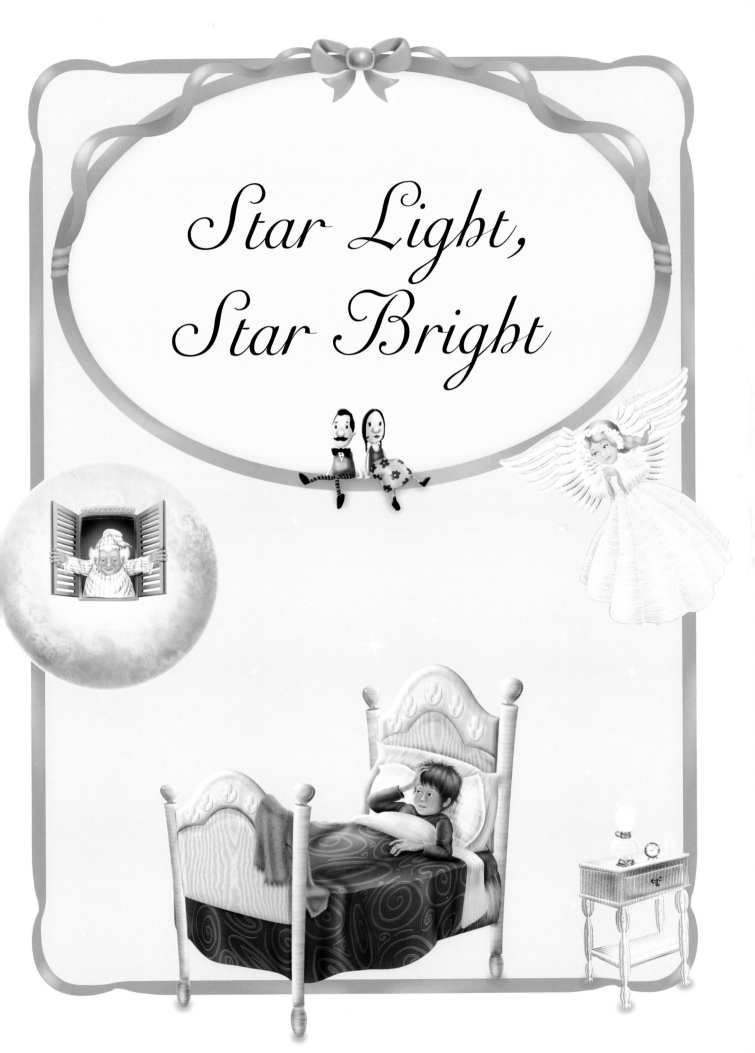

STAR WISH

Star light, star bright,
First star I see tonight,
I wish I may, I wish I might,
Have the wish I wish tonight.

GOODNIGHT, SLEEP TIGHT

Goodnight, sleep tight,
  Wake up bright
In the morning light,
To do what's right
With all your might.

BRAHMS' LULLABY

Lullaby and goodnight,
With roses bestride,
With lilies bedecked,
'Neath baby's sweet bed.

May thou sleep, may thou rest,
May thy slumber be blest.
May thou sleep, may thou rest,
May thy slumber be blest.

Lullaby and goodnight,
Thy mother's delight.
Bright angels around,
My darling, shall guard.

They will guide thee from harm,
Thou art safe in my arms.
They will guide thee from harm,
Thou art safe in my arms.

Johannes Brahms